Love

Emma Dodd

nosy™
crow

An imprint of Candlewick Press

Love is in the morning when
you wake and smile at me.

Love is when we talk together, happy as can be.

Sometimes love is quiet
and it needs no words at all.

Love is there
to catch you
when you are
about to fall.

Love is when we huddle close
and shelter from a shower.

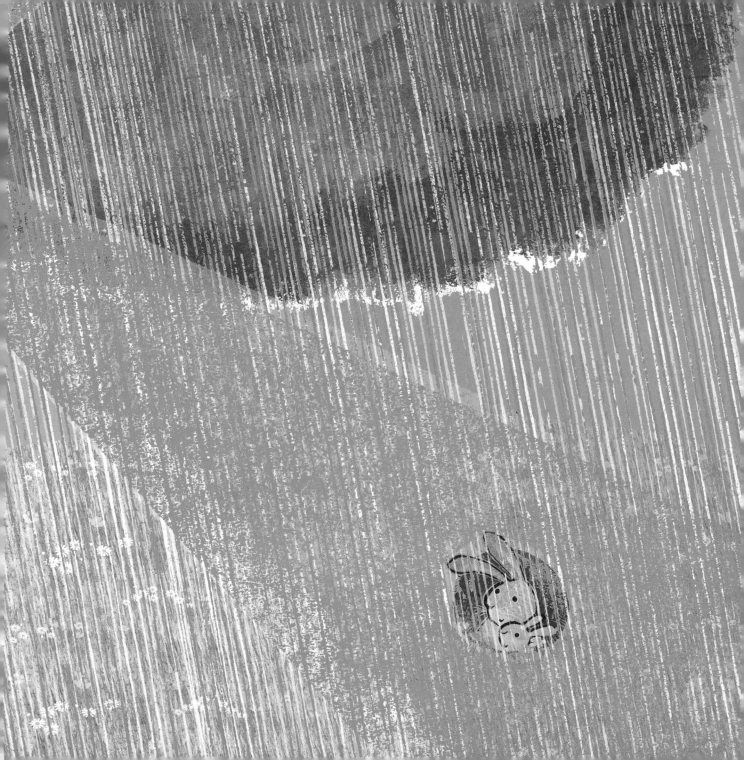

Love is when
we take the
time to stop and
smell a flower.

I love you when you get it right
and when you get it wrong.

The world is
much more lovely
since the day you
came along.

I love you so,

and when I try to count

the reasons why . . .

I find there are more reasons . . .

than there are

stars up in the sky.

First U.S. edition 2016

Library of Congress Catalog Card Number 2015941805
ISBN 978-0-7636-8941-4

17 18 19 20 21 GBL 10 9 8 7 6 5

Printed in Shenzhen, Guangdong, China

This book was typeset in Eureka Sans.
The illustrations were created digitally.

Nosy Crow
an imprint of
Candlewick Press
99 Dover Street
Somerville, Massachusetts 02144

www.nosycrow.com
www.candlewick.com